Jan Ormerod

grew up in Australia and since 1982 has illustrated
over 60 children's books. Her first picture book, *Sunshine*,
won the Mother Goose Award and was Highly Commended
for the Kate Greenaway Medal. Her books for Frances Lincoln
include *A Twist in the Tail – Animal Stories from Around the World*,
written by Mary Hoffman, *Ponko and the South Pole*,
written by Meredith Hooper, and the classic wordless
picture books *Sunshine* and *Moonlight*.

For Jana Novotny Hunter

When an Elephant Comes to School copyright © Frances Lincoln Limited 2004
Text and illustrations copyright © Jan Ormerod 2004

The Publishers would like to thank Hannah Shone, aged 10, for the beautiful hand-lettering in this book.

First published in Great Britain in 2004 by Frances Lincoln Children's Books,
4 Torriano Mews, Torriano Avenue, London NW5 2RZ

www.franceslincoln.com

First paperback edition published in 2005

British Library Cataloguing in Publication Data available on request

ISBN 1-84507-431-9

Printed in Singapore
1 3 5 7 9 8 6 4 2

When an Elephant Comes to School

Jan Ormerod

FRANCES LINCOLN CHILDREN'S BOOKS

Arriving at School

When an elephant comes to school…

he may be a bit shy at first. A special friend
can show him where to put his lunch-box.

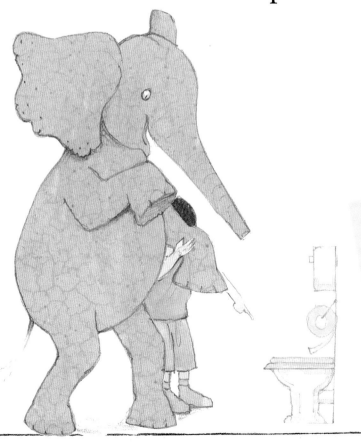

Show ☆
him the
toilets
right away.

Making Friends

Friends are very important
to an elephant.

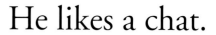

He likes a chat.

He loves to play.

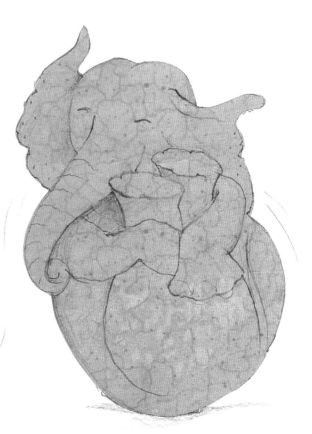

An elephant wants
to join in everything.

An elephant
needs lots
of love
and cuddles
and hugs.
☆

Messy Moments

An elephant loves…

paint,

A plastic apron is a good idea. ☆

water,

glue,

and sand.

Keep a dustpan and brush near the Sandtray.

Carrying

An elephant loves to carry things...

especially his friends.

An elephant loves to experiment.

Whoops!

An elephant can be a bit clumsy…

and elephants
are not very brave.

When he falls over, make a big fuss of him. ☆

Yum-Yum

An elephant loves to eat.

Best of all he likes cake,
bananas and lemonade.

Take
an extra
sandwich.
☆

Playtime

Elephants are good at doing tricks with a ball.

Don't let an elephant step on your toes. ☆

But…

elephants are NOT
good at sharing.

Quiet Times

If he gets cross,
he is probably
tired and thirsty.

An elephant needs
lots and lots of rest.

A quiet time with a book
and a sensible friend
is a good idea.

He likes
stories
about other
elephants.
☆

TRA·LA·LA

An elephant loves music.
He likes to dance...

and march.

An elephant loves to play a tambourine. ☆

An elephant loves a funny story...

Have a
big box
of tissues
ready.
☆

but a sad story makes him cry.

He likes to make up
his own stories.

Bye-Bye

When an elephant comes to school
he loves to make friends and have fun
learning things.

And he loves to see his mummy
at the end of the day.

"See you tomorrow, Elephant!"

MORE TITLES WITH JAN ORMEROD FROM FRANCES LINCOLN

Sunshine

It's morning and the first rays of sunlight
shine into a little girl's bedroom and wake her up.
She gets out of bed, goes to wake her parents
and soon she is ready to start the day.

ISBN 1-84507-390-8

Moonlight

It's nearly bedtime and a little girl
is eating her dinner, playing in the bath and saying good night
to her dollies. But she's not quite ready to sleep yet…

ISBN 1-84507-391-6

Ponko and the South Pole

Meredith Hooper
Illustrated by Jan Ormerod

This delightful story follows Ponko the Penguin
and his friend Joey Bear as they stow away on a sledge to take part
in the Great Expedition to the South Pole.
Based on the real toy penguin called Ponko who belonged
to the famous Antarctic explorer and photographer,
Herbert Ponting.

ISBN 1-84507-016-X

Frances Lincoln titles are available from all good bookshops.
You can also buy books and find out more about your favourite titles,
authors and illustrators on our website: www.franceslincoln.com